MICKEY MANTLE

by Bill Morgan

♦ *Classic Sports Shots* ♦

SCHOLASTIC INC.
New York • Toronto • London • Auckland • Sydney

ISBN 0-590-47024-8

12 11 10 9 8 7 6 5 4 3 2 1   3 4 5 6 7 8/9

Printed in the U.S.A.   10

First Scholastic printing, January 1993

CONTENTS

Mickey holds three bats — one for each home run he hit against Detroit in a 1955 game.

CHAPTER ONE

GROWING UP

The first clothes Mickey Mantle remembers wearing as a child were made from his father's baseball uniforms. His father, Elvin C. Mantle, known as Mutt, worked in a lead mine in northern Oklahoma during the week. But on weekends, he satisfied his passion for baseball by playing in a semiprofessional league. When his uniforms got ripped, Mickey's mother, Lovell, made them into clothes for her children.

Mutt was an all-around baseball player. He was able to bat from both sides of the plate and could play any position, including pitcher. Mutt spent a lot of time teaching his son the game.

"I wanted to make Mickey into a ballplayer ever since he was born. I guess I put a glove on his hand when he was just a little-bitty kid," said Mickey's father.

Mickey Charles Mantle was born on October 20, 1931, in the small town of Spavinaw, Oklahoma. The Mantles lived in a two-room house.

It was a difficult time for many people who lived in Oklahoma. The Great Depression was causing many Oklahoma farmers to lose their farms because they couldn't make a living. Many packed up their families and moved to California, looking for a better life.

The Mantle family moved, too. But not to California. Mutt got a job in a lead mine in Commerce, a mining town in northeast Oklahoma, close to the Missouri border.

It was in Commerce that Mickey learned to play, and love, baseball. His grandfather loved baseball as much as Mutt, and the two older Mantle men would spend hours teaching Mickey how to play. Mutt wanted Mickey to be able to hit the ball from both sides of the plate like he could.

Mickey's father would pitch to his son while Mickey batted from the left side of the plate, and his grandfather would pitch to him while he batted from the right. It was behind an old tin barn that the young Mickey learned how to become a switch-hitter — before he ever played in a game.

When he was old enough to play in games, he batted left-handed against a

Mickey and his first Yankee manager, Casey Stengel.

right-handed pitcher and right-handed against a southpaw.

On weekends, Mickey watched his father play. He imagined he was watching a major league game and his father was the great catcher of the day, Mickey Cochrane — the man Mutt had named his son after.

It wasn't long before Mickey and a couple of his friends were hiking three miles to play sandlot baseball in a nearby town. "We would have walked a hundred miles to show up for practice," Mickey remembers.

Games between neighboring mining towns were played on weekends, and families would make a day of it to watch. Mickey remembers how families spread out picnic lunches and cheered for their favorite team. The young players felt like they were in the World Series.

When Mickey was in junior high school, Mutt stopped working in the mine because the dust from the mine was coating his lungs. He traded the Mantle house in Commerce for some cows, a horse, farm equipment, and the right to work 160 acres on a local farm. The Mantles moved into a small house on the farm property and worked the land for the family that owned it.

Mutt liked being in the outdoors, and the Mantle kids — Mickey and his younger sister and brothers, — Barbara, Ray, Roy, and Butch — played baseball and football in the large yard. Mickey rode a horse to school, hitched it to a post, and rode it home at the end of the day. On Saturdays he often went to see westerns at the local movie house, and to a local restaurant where he paid 25 cents for a hamburger, bowl of chili, and soda.

Before Mickey started high school, disaster struck. Four days of rain ruined the crop that Mutt had been cultivating all summer. The Mantles had to give up life on the farm, and Mutt had to go back to work in the lead mine.

The family moved to a small shack in a tiny village just outside of Commerce. There was no indoor plumbing, and Mickey had to share a bedroom with his parents and his sister, Barbara.

Times were hard for the Mantle family, but they survived. And Mickey continued to play baseball.

An early publicity photo of Mickey in his Yankee pinstripes.

CHAPTER TWO

HIGH SCHOOL

By the time Mickey was a student at Commerce High, he was obsessed with sports. He played halfback for the school's football team.

His father was not too pleased. He was afraid that Mickey would get hurt and wouldn't be able to play baseball. And it turned out that he was right.

At practice one day during the 1946 season, a player kicked Mickey in the left shin while trying to tackle him. Mickey had to be carried off the field. That night he ran a fever of 104 degrees and had to be taken to the hospital. His left ankle was swollen. When the swelling didn't go down after two weeks, the doctor told Mickey's mother that Mickey had an infection in the ankle and the leg might have to be amputated.

Mickey's parents immediately moved him to the Crippled Children's Center in Oklahoma City. A new drug, penicillin, had just come out. Mickey was given an injection of the drug every three hours. Soon the ankle began to improve and, finally, he was allowed to return home. But for months, Mickey was confined to bed. He had to rest so the infection wouldn't come back.

However, the next summer, Mickey was playing sandlot baseball again. He played with every team he could. Every time he played he had just one purpose — to get better.

His enthusiasm for sports also helped him get a job on the school paper. Mrs. Aldene Campbell made Mickey an editor. He covered sports. Mrs. Campbell sent him to a competition for high school journalism students, who were given tests, and Mickey came in second.

But it was playing sports, rather than writing about them, that Mickey loved most. During the summer of 1947, he began playing organized baseball.

A man named Barney Barrett organized a league that played near Commerce. Although it wasn't professional, the players were better than those who played sandlot ball. Professional scouts from the major leagues would sometimes show up, looking for prospects.

Mickey met Barney when Barney's team, the Whiz Kids of Baxter Springs, played Mickey's team. Barney liked what he saw when he watched Mickey play and asked him to join the Whiz Kids next season. All winter long, Mickey dreamed about playing for the Whiz Kids, who were the best team in the league.

But first Mickey had to get through another school year, which meant another year of sports — but not football. Mickey decided to join the Commerce High basketball team. His mother went to every game. She loved to cheer for her son as he ran up and down the court. She also yelled at the referees when they made a call against Commerce that she didn't like. It got so bad that Mickey's father would sit a couple of rows away from her because he was embarrassed.

The summer of 1948 arrived, and Mickey played shortstop for Baxter Springs. There were games almost every night.

One night Mickey hit three home runs. The fans decided to pass the hat for Mickey to show their appreciation. Fifty-three dollars had been collected when the hat was given to Mickey. It was more money than he had ever seen and about what his father made in two weeks, working in the mine.

But somebody called the Oklahoma Athletic Commission and told them that Mickey was still a high school athlete, so he had to give the money back to Barrett.

Mickey did have a summer job, though. By day he worked at a cemetery in Baxter Springs, digging graves and putting up tombstones. And at night he played baseball.

It was during this summer of 1948, before Mickey's senior year at Commerce High, that Tom Greenwade, a scout from the New York Yankees, came to see the

Whiz Kids play. He actually came to see another player but was impressed when he saw Mickey hit homers from both the left and right sides of the plate.

When a rainstorm halted the game and everyone was running for cover, Mutt grabbed Mickey and told him a scout for the Yankees wanted to talk to him. Greenwade asked him if he wanted to play for the Yankees. Mickey was speechless.

Greenwade couldn't offer him a contract because Mickey had another year of high school. But the scout promised to return on his graduation day from Commerce High.

If Mickey had dreamed about playing for the Whiz Kids the year before, it was nothing compared to dreaming about playing for the Yankees as he attended classes his senior year.

True to his word, Greenwade showed

up when Mickey graduated. But Mickey didn't go to the graduation ceremony. He was playing for the Whiz Kids that night.

Greenwade offered him a contract to play for Independence, Kansas, in a Class D league, and Mickey signed.

Mutt drove Mickey to Independence, and the two Mantle men met the manager of the team, Harry Craft. "I've done all I can for Mickey. I believe he's a good ballplayer," Mutt said to the manager. "Now I'm turning him over to you."

An 18-year-old Mickey, when he was playing in Joplin, Missouri, in the Yankee minor league farm system.

CHAPTER THREE

THE MINOR LEAGUES

At 17 years of age, Mickey was beginning his professional baseball career, and he was nervous. He was in a new town, with new people, and his father wouldn't be around to offer his support.

And his first few weeks of playing for Independence didn't help. Mickey was having a hard time at shortstop and wasn't doing much better at the plate. He thought about going back to Commerce and working in the mine with his father.

Harry Craft took Mickey under his wing

and encouraged him not to dwell on his mistakes. Soon Mickey's playing improved, and he got used to the long bus rides that took the team to games in Kansas, Missouri, and Oklahoma.

Independence won the league championship, and after the season, Mickey returned to Commerce. He got a job at the mine, driving a truck.

One Friday night, Mickey went to a local high school football game with a friend. His friend was dating one of the majorettes, a girl named Pat Johnson. Her sister, Merlyn, was also a majorette. After the game, Mickey and his friend went out with the two girls.

A week later, Mickey called Merlyn and asked her for a date. They went to the movies, and he asked her for another date. She said yes, and Mickey took her to another movie. That fall of 1949,

Mickey and Merlyn began to go out on a lot of dates.

In January 1950, Mickey signed a contract to play Class C ball in Joplin, Missouri. When he arrived at Joplin, he was surprised to see that the ballpark was old and not in very good condition. There were rocks in the outfield that players would pick up and put in their pockets between innings.

There was a local orphanage behind right field. During the season, Mickey hit several home runs in that direction, including one that broke a window.

The next day when Mickey came up to bat, he noticed that a huge bed sheet was hanging out one of the windows. It said THANKS FOR THE BALL, MICKEY.

Mickey had a great season. He led the league in runs scored (141), hits (199), and batting average (.383). Just before the season ended, Craft pulled Mickey aside. The manager told him that the Yankees were calling him up to finish the season with them.

On September 17, 1950, Mickey joined the Yankees for a doubleheader they were playing in St. Louis. He watched Yankee stars like Phil Rizutto and Joe DiMaggio take infield and batting practice. He couldn't believe he was actually there and was too shy to talk to his heroes. He didn't get into any Yankee games that fall.

When the season ended, Mickey returned to Commerce and again worked at the mine and dated Merlyn. One night, while passing a jewelry store, Mickey and Merlyn went in. Merlyn tried on a ring for fun, and on the spur of the moment, Mickey asked her to marry him. She said yes, but they didn't set a wedding date.

In January 1951, Mickey got a letter telling him to report to the Yankee spring training camp in Phoenix, Arizona, in February. Since there was no train ticket with the letter, he figured he would hear from the team again.

But he didn't. The middle of February arrived, and he was still working in the mine. One day a local sportswriter showed up and told Mickey that the Yankees had called, asking why Mickey wasn't at spring training. Mickey told the sportswriter that he hadn't received a train ticket.

Mickey ran to the mining office and placed a collect call to the Yankees. The next day a train ticket arrived, and that night he left for Phoenix. As the train departed, Mickey knew that a new phase in his life was beginning. He was going to be a New York Yankee.

The famous Mantle swing.

♦22

CHAPTER FOUR

THE MAJOR LEAGUES

Some of the players, including Joe DiMaggio and Billy Martin, were at camp when Mickey arrived. Even though Mickey had enjoyed a great season in Joplin and the New York sportswriters were beginning to call him the next DiMaggio, he didn't speak to any of the Yankee stars unless they said something to him.

Mickey began spring training working out at shortstop. The Yankees thought his skills as a shortstop were limited and didn't see him becoming the team's first-stringer — especially with Phil Rizzuto already at the position.

But the Yanks were impressed with Mickey's speed. Manager Casey Stengel timed him as he ran around the bases. He did it in just under 13 seconds. Stengel wanted that speed in his outfield and put Mickey in right field.

In Mickey's first exhibition game, against Cleveland, Ray Boone lined a drive at Mickey in the outfield. He flipped his sunglasses down but, all of a sudden, he was in total darkness. The ball hit him on the forehead.

Luckily, Mickey improved as an outfielder. And he impressed the Yankee coaches with his hitting. By the end of the exhibition season, he was hitting .402 and traveling on the train to Washington, D.C., to play for the Yankees in their season's opening game.

The series in Washington was rained out, so Mickey played his first game as a Yankee in New York in front of 50,000 people. All he could think about was the fact that there were only 2,500 people in all of Commerce, Oklahoma!

Mickey got his first major league hit — a single — in the sixth inning. As he stood on first base, he thought about all of the great baseball players who had played in the Stadium: Babe Ruth, Lou Gehrig, and Joe DiMaggio, to name a few.

If Mickey felt the presence of those players on the field, he was pretty lonely off the field. He lived in a hotel near the Stadium and sat alone many nights. or went to a diner for a meal. He missed his family and Merlyn back in Commerce.

Not long into the season, Mickey went into a slump. Then he made a few errors in the outfield. In July, Casey sent him to

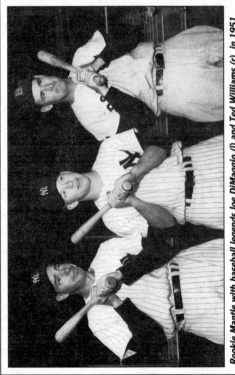

Rookie Mantle with baseball legends Joe DiMaggio (l) and Ted Williams (r), in 1951.

the Yankees' Triple-A minor league team in Kansas City.

Mickey didn't do much better in Kansas City and began to feel sorry for himself. He called his father in Commerce and told Mutt that he wanted to quit. His father told him he was on his way.

Five hours later, Mutt knocked on the door of Mickey's hotel room. Mickey still remembers what his father said: "Mickey, if that's all the guts you got, pack up and come home with me now and be a miner."

Mickey thought about what his father had said. "After he went home," said Mickey years later, "I couldn't do anything wrong. I hit about 15 home runs and knocked in 55, 56 runs in three weeks, and they brought me back to New York."

The Yankees met the Giants, who then

played in New York, in the 1951 World Series, and Mickey started the first two games. In the second game, while going for a ball in the outfield, Mickey stopped running when center fielder Joe DiMaggio called for it. Mickey's foot caught on a drainpipe, and he went down, injuring his right knee.

The next morning the knee hurt so much that he had to go to the hospital. Mutt had come to New York for the Series. When he put his arm around Mickey to help him out of the cab, Mutt collapsed on the sidewalk.

The Mantle men ended up sharing a room at the hospital. Mickey needed to have torn ligaments in his knee operated on. The news about Mutt was worse. He had cancer, and the doctor informed Mickey that nothing could be done. Mutt was dying.

Mickey and his wife, Merlyn.

When Mickey returned to Commerce that fall, he bought a seven-room house for his family. The cast stayed on his knee till November. On December 23, 1951, Mickey and Merlyn got married.

Mickey reported to spring training for the 1952 season worried about his knee. So were the Yankees. Mickey played in a few exhibition games and, by the start of the season, felt that he could play full time.

DiMaggio had retired, so the Yankees were looking for someone to replace him in center field. The leading contenders were Mickey and Jackie Jensen. Stengel gave each man starts at the position as the 1952 season began.

On May 6, Mickey got a call that his father had died. He played in a game against Cleveland that night and then left to attend the funeral in Commerce.

Back in New York after Mutt's funeral, Mickey caught fire and became the starting center fielder. He also got a new roommate when the Yankees were on the road — Billy Martin.

Mickey and Billy became fast friends and often got into trouble. On the field, both players were all business, but off the field, their business was playing. They loved to go to parties and nightclubs. Sometimes teammate Whitey Ford would join them, but it was usually Mickey and Billy who started the parties.

Sometimes things got so bad that Yankees general manager George Weiss would fine Mickey and Billy for staying out past the players' curfew. But the fines didn't stop them.

Despite their antics, they helped the Yankees win the World Series in 1952. Mickey hit over .300 for the first time

(.311), with 23 homers and 87 RBIs.

After the season, Mickey and Merlyn settled into a new home in Commerce. Meryln was expecting their first child when Mickey left for spring training in February 1953.

At an exhibition game in Brooklyn, just before the season started, Mickey stepped up to the plate as the announcer told the crowd — and Mickey — that Mickey was the new father of a baby boy. He didn't get to see Mickey Jr. until a month later when he went back to Commerce for a few days.

Early in the season, Mickey hit a historic home run at Griffith Stadium in Washington, D.C. The ball went out of the stadium and landed in someone's backyard. Someone left the press box, found it, and measured the distance from home plate — 565 feet. The next day, the papers said the home run was the longest in major league history.

Mickey averaged around .300 in the 1954 and 1955 seasons, which were just warm-ups for what would be his greatest year, 1956.

In 1956, Mickey became only the fourth player in history to lead both leagues in batting average (.353), home runs (52), and runs batted in (130). Mickey won baseball's triple crown, was the American League's Most Valuable Player, and was named Player of the Year by *The Sporting News.*

After the season, Mickey and Merlyn moved to Dallas. Merlyn had given birth to another son, David, before the 1956 season, and the house in Commerce was now too small for their growing family.

In 1957 Mickey hit .365 and won his second consecutive MVP award. For

Mickey it was another great season.

Except for one thing. General manager Weiss finally got tired of the antics of Billy Martin, Mickey's good friend and fellow cutup, and traded Billy to Kansas City. Mickey still had Whitey Ford, but he missed Billy. The two men spent a lot of time together in the off-season, even after they were no longer teammates.

For the next three seasons, Mickey continued to be the most powerful switch-hitter in the major leagues and one of the most feared hitters in baseball. In 1960 Mickey led the American League with 40 home runs. A fellow Yankee, Roger Maris, hit 39.

Mickey has said that 1956 was his favorite summer. But the one most fans remember was the home-run derby between Mickey and Roger Maris during the 1961 season.

Roger Maris (l) and Mickey during the great home-run derby of 1961.

In 1927 Babe Ruth hit 60 home runs, one baseball record many people thought would never be broken. By midseason in 1961, both Mickey and Roger were well ahead of the Babe's record home-run pace. The press began to go wild. Everywhere the Yankees played, reporters wanted to talk to the two home-run hitters and ask them if they thought they could break the record. There wasn't a moment's peace for either Yankee.

Finally the Yankees found an apartment the two men could share so reporters wouldn't know where they lived. It was the only time both men had any peace and quiet.

Mickey led the race for most of the season but was felled by a bad cold in early September. He finished the season with 54, while Roger went on to break The Babe's record, hitting 61.

For the next three seasons, Mickey continued to terrorize American League pitchers. He won his third MVP award in 1962. But he also injured himself, pulling a muscle in his right thigh. When he fell to the ground, he damaged his left knee. Now both of his knees had been injured. And for the rest of his career, he would feel constant pain when playing.

Even so, Mickey continued to hit over .300 in the 1963 and 1964 seasons.

The 1965 season saw Mickey hit only .255, his lowest average in his major league career. The Yankees were beginning to slide, too. After a first-place finish in 1964, the Yanks fell to sixth in 1965.

During the off-season, Mickey hurt his right shoulder, playing touch football, and had to undergo surgery. While the shoulder never felt as good as before the injury, Mickey was able to play in 1966 and raised his average to .288.

During spring training of 1967, Mickey was moved to first base. His knees continued to bother him, and it was difficult for him to chase after long fly balls. By 1968, it hurt just to stand at first base.

Before one game in Cleveland, Mickey's legs hurt so badly that he couldn't play. After the game, a man came up to Mickey and told him that he had brought his son 400 miles to see the game and was so disappointed because Mickey hadn't played. That's when Mickey knew that retirement was near.

He reported to spring training for the 1969 season, but after trying to work out a couple of times, Mickey knew it was time to leave the game he loved so much.

On March 1, 1969, he made the announcement: "I can't hit anymore," said Mickey at a press conference.

On June 8, 1969, the Yankees held Mickey Mantle Day at the Stadium. More than 60,000 fans stood and cheered for the kid from Commerce. His number — seven — was retired, and Mickey talked about life after baseball.

"The thing I miss the most is being around the clubhouse. I've got some guys on this team that are almost like brothers to me," Mickey told the crowd.

His Yankee teammates felt that they had lost a brother. Six teammates from his 18-year Yankee career had even named their sons Mickey.

In 1974 Mickey was elected to the Baseball Hall of Fame in his first year of eligibility. One of his fellow inductees was his friend and teammate Whitey Ford. "Along with having my number retired on Mickey Mantle Day, going into the Hall of Fame with Whitey has to be the biggest

Mickey says thanks to fans at Yankee Stadium on June 8, 1969, after his retirement from baseball.

moment in my life," Mickey said.

After he retired from baseball, Mickey made some investments — from a men's clothing line to a chain of fast-food restaurants. Not all were successful. "I invested like I hit — a lot of strikeouts," Mickey says with a laugh today.

One investment that has paid off is his restaurant in New York City called Mickey Mantle's. It is a favorite of athletes, fans, and lovers of good home-style cooking.

Of course, with retirement came time to spend with Merlyn and his four boys, Mickey Jr., David, Billy, and Danny. The Mantles still reside in Dallas in the house that Mickey purchased in 1957. He spends time playing golf and doing charity work.

When he is in New York, he has dinner at his restaurant and loves talking to fans. He also knows that families often

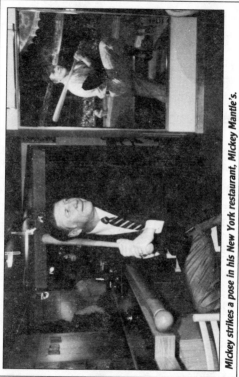

Mickey strikes a pose in his New York restaurant, Mickey Mantle's.

come in to see him. It soon became apparent that some people couldn't afford to feed their kids when the only things on the menu were expensive adult meals. Mickey introduced a Little League menu so kids had something more to their liking while hoping to see the former Yankee superstar.

For many Americans, Mickey Mantle will always be one of the greatest baseball players who ever lived. He had 2,415 hits and hit 536 home runs. His career batting average was .298. Mickey played with a spirit and determination that is not always seen in today's players.

NBC sportscaster Bob Costas remembers watching Mantle and still, to this day, carries Mickey's baseball card in his wallet. His opinion of Mickey Mantle is simply, "He is one of the biggest heroes this country has ever had."

CAREER HIGHLIGHTS

- Was a three-time American League Most Valuable Player (1956, 1957, 1962).
- Won baseball's triple crown for leading the majors in batting average (.353), home runs (52), and runs batted in (130), in 1956.
- Was a member of 12 American League pennant-winning teams (1951–53, 1955–58, 1960-64).
- Was a member of seven World Series championship teams (1951–53, 1956, 1958, 1961– 62).
- Had his uniform number — seven — retired at a Yankee Stadium ceremony on June 8, 1969.
- Was elected into baseball's Hall of Fame in his first year of eligibility (1974).